OUTSIDE AND INSIDE

BATS

BY SANDRA MARKLE

ATHENEUM BOOKS FOR YOUNG READERS

In memory of Edythe Louys, who encouraged and inspired me.

The author would especially like to thank the following for sharing their enthusiasm and expertise: Thomas Kunz, Boston University and Susan Barnard, Zoo Atlanta. And a special thanks to my assistant, Contance Parramore, whose creativity and resourcefulness added significantly to the development of *Outside and Inside Bats*.

ATHENEUM BOOKS FOR YOUNG READERS
An imprint of Simon & Schuster Children's Publishing Division
1230 Avenue of the Americas
New York, New York 10020

Book design by Anne Scatto/PIXEL PRESS
The text of this book is set in 15.5 pt Melior
First edition
Printed in Singapore
10   9   8   7   6   5   4

Library of Congress Cataloging-in-Publication Data:
Markle, Sandra.
Outside and inside bats / by Sandra Markle.—1st ed.
p.   cm.
Includes index.
Summary: Describes the inner and outer workings of bats, discussing their diet, anatomy, and reproduction.
ISBN 0-689-81165-9
1. Bats—Juvenile literature. 2. Bats—Anatomy—Juvenile literature.
[1. Bats.] I. Title.
QL737.C5M36   1997
599.4—dc21
96-48291
CIP   AC

NOTE: To help readers pronounce words that may not be familiar to them, pronunciations are given in the glossary/index. Glossary words are italicized the first time they appear.

TITLE PAGE: *Lesser long-nosed bats*

Look at this Sanborn's long-nosed bat swooping into the flower. Do you ever wonder why bats can fly and you can't? This book will let you take a close look at bats—outside and inside—and find out.

THUMB

One thing a bat has that you do not is *wings*. These are not like bird wings, though. Bird wings are feathers stuck to a frame that opens and folds. Bat wings are skin stretched over a hand that bends as freely as your fingers. So a bat can easily change its wing shape to turn, hover, and do flips.

There are two main groups of bats: one that depends on sight and smell to find food, and another that depends on hearing to locate food. Wing shape and wingspan—the distance from wingtip to wingtip—vary with the kind and size of bat. The smallest bat, Thailand's bumblebee bat, has a wingspan that is probably smaller than you can spread one hand. The biggest bat, Southeast Asia's flying fox, has a wingspan slightly longer than the average bathtub.

OPPOSITE: *Look closely at this long-eared* <u>Myotis</u> *and you will see something you and a bat share—a movable thumb. Think of all the things you do with your thumb, and you'll know how useful having a movable thumb is for the bat.*

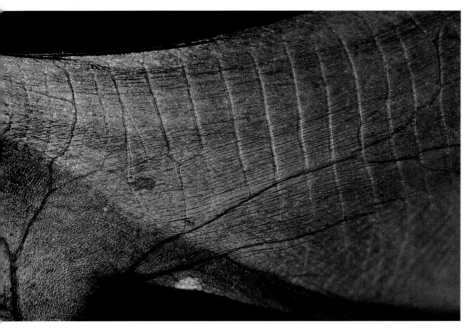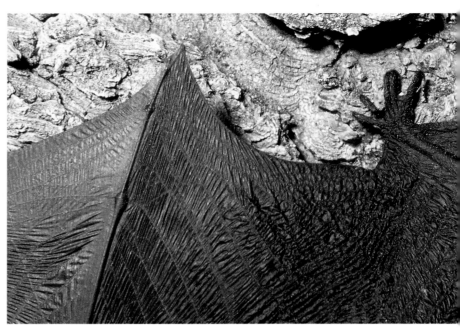

OUTSTRETCHED WING   PARTLY FOLDED WING

The red lines are blood vessels, carrying blood throughout the wing. You can read more about what blood does on page 26.

Examine part of a bat's wing stretched for flight. This *membrane* is mainly an upper and a lower layer of skin. It is so thin you can see through it. Because a torn or damaged wing would make flight impossible, bats are careful to avoid running into things. When hunting for food in a group, bats avoid bumping into each other by making sounds, the way cars honk at each other on a busy highway.

Next, look at the partly folded wing. The puckers form because there are hundreds of groups of tiny *muscles* between the two layers of membrane. When its wings are not in use, a bat folds them to protect the membrane. And the muscles gather up the elastic skin like pulling up a window shade, so there are no exposed loose flaps.

See how completely this red bat's wings are folded to protect the delicate membrane? Bats that are awake spend a lot of time using their *tongue,* teeth, and toenails to groom their wing membranes and hair. They use their thumb like a cotton-tipped swab to clean out their ears.

All bats have hair on their bodies, although two kinds of a group called naked bats have only a little fuzz. Some have hair extending over the back side of the wings to protect the skin as well as to help keep them warm and dry. Hair color also helps the red bat hide from enemies, like owls and hawks, by making it look like a dead leaf.

The red bat has a furry tail it uses much the way you would wrap up in a blanket.

BAT HAIR

Now, look at this close-up picture of hair from a big brown bat. How is it like human hair? How is it different?

In addition to normal body hair, some bats also have special hairs. Body parts called *glands* at the base of these hairs produce scented juices. Then the clusters of hairs trap these scents. The scent of this "perfume" may help the bat attract a mate. Males of some kinds of bats have glands under their chin and even on the wing membrane. They use their hair like a paintbrush to wipe on scent droplets, marking their *roosting* place or their mate.

HUMAN HAIR

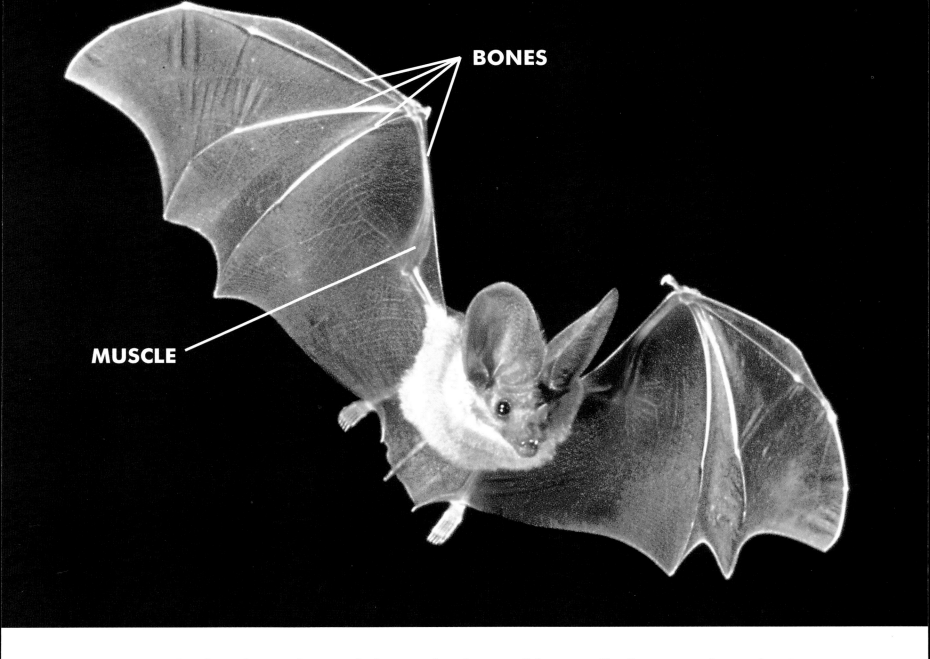

BONES

MUSCLE

Look closely at this California leaf-nosed bat in flight. Wonder what's under its hair and supporting those outstretched wings? *Bones,* for one thing. You can easily see some of the bones in the wings.

9

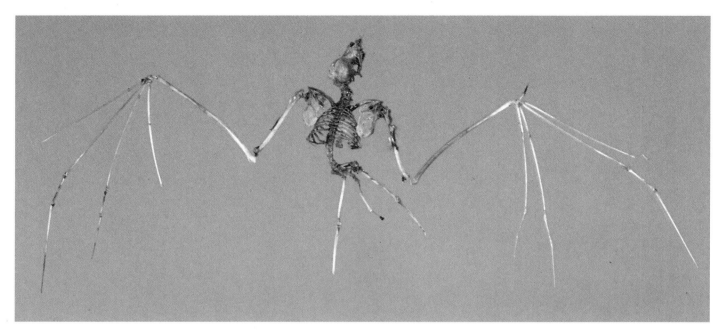

Examine this skeleton of a common bent-winged bat. Compare its arms and hands, backbone, and legs to yours.

Squeeze your arm and pat your knees to feel the bones inside. Like you, a bat has a hard, bony inside framework, or *skeleton,* that gives its body shape. Now bend your fingers, arms, and legs. The body can only bend where bones meet. The bat's body, like yours, is made up of different kinds of bones.

Imagine having fingers as long as a bat's! Those fingers, like the spokes of an umbrella, support and stretch out the wing membrane for flight. Muscles power movement by pulling on the bones. Look back at the California leaf-nosed bat to see the muscles that move the bat's upper arm to flap its wing.

Now, check out the bat's neck bones. Like you, a bat has seven neck bones. Tip your head back as far as you can, and you'll be able to look straight overhead. If your neck was as flexible as some bats, you could arch your neck enough to look behind you. Bats able to move their necks this way have neck bones shaped to rotate as freely as your arm does at the shoulder. This lets a bat that is hanging upside down lift its head to eat or to look around.

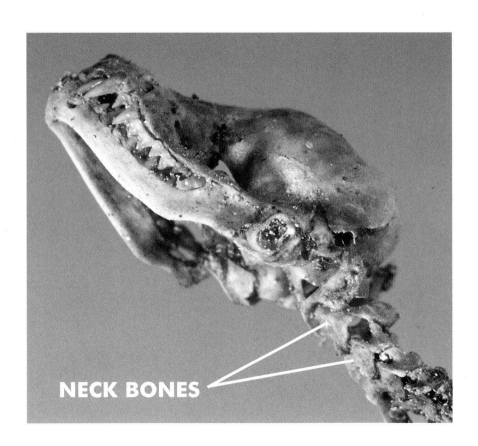

NECK BONES

See how the bat's wings are more curved above than below? Holding its wings in this sail shape helps give the bat *lift,* the force it needs to stay in the air. To understand how this shape adds lift, try this. Cut a strip of newspaper about five centimeters (two inches) wide and fifteen centimeters (six inches) long. Holding the long edges, put one short end against your lower lip. Blow hard on the paper. The free end will rise.

By blowing, you made the air on the upper surface of the paper move quickly. As the fast-flowing air moves away, it sucks the paper up. At the same time, the slower-moving air on the lower surface pushes up, helping lift the paper.

Air tends to slide faster over the curved upper surface of a bat's wings than the lower surface. This air sucks the wings upward, while the slower-moving air under the wings pushes up. Several pairs of muscles work together so the bat can flap its wings. Weaker back muscles raise the wings, and then strong chest muscles power the downward sweep. Flapping makes more air flow over a bat's wings. With a sort of swimming motion similar to the butterfly stroke, the downstroke propels the bat forward.

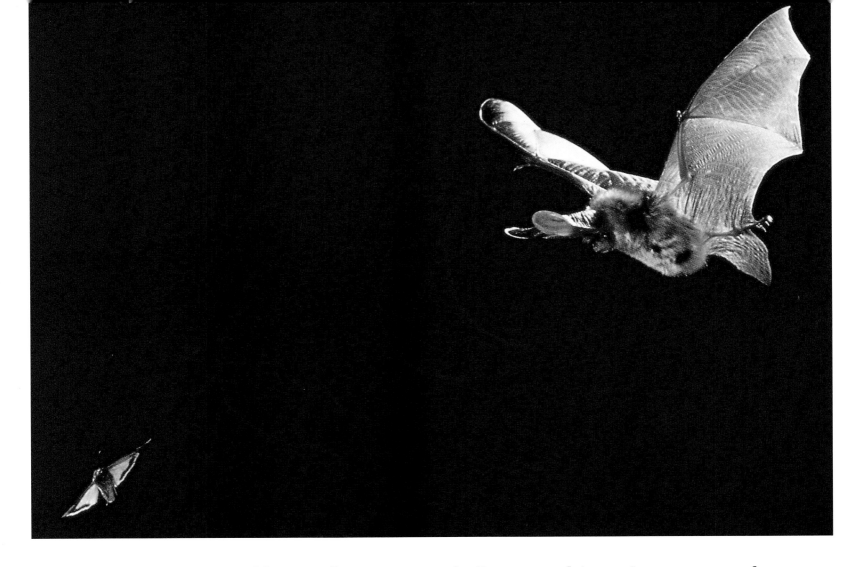

This long-eared bat is chasing a moth. Because this action was caught with a special camera flash you can see both the bat and the moth. In real life, the bat would be swooping through the dark in search of a bug meal. How do you think it could find the moth at night when it is too dark to see clearly?

Clue: Close your eyes and listen for a sound. Can you point to the source of that sound?

Townsend's big-eared bat

Did you guess the bat uses its big ears? Sounds are moving waves of air, and big ears help a bat "catch" sound waves and direct them to sound-sensitive *cells* inside the bat's ear. Signals from these cells are sent to the *brain.* The brain figures out the messages, and the bat hears. Not all bats wait to hear sounds, though. Some make their own sounds and then listen for echoes as the sounds bounce off a rock, a tree, a bug, or another bat and return to them. Using sounds this way is called *echolocation,* and it lets the bat's brain develop a sort of sound picture. This allows the bat to steer safely and hunt even when it is pitch dark.

Whistle, click your tongue against the roof of your mouth, and snort through your nose. These are the ways different kinds of bats send out sound signals, but most bat calls are so high-pitched your ears cannot hear the sounds. Those calling through their nose, like the bat on page 4, usually have flaps of skin called *nose leaves* around the nose to direct the sound forward. Leaf-nosed bats produce sounds through their nose because many feed on insects or fruit they carry in their mouth.

If you could peek inside a bat's head while it was sending out its sounds, you would discover something interesting happening. Just as the bat calls, muscles squeeze its middle ear. Like pressing your hands over your ears, this protects the bat's ears from being deafened by its own sound blast. As soon as the call ends, the muscles relax and the bat is ready to listen for the echo. Since the bat is listening for its own voice, it is usually not confused by other sounds. For some bats, having sound reach one ear slightly ahead of the other lets them locate the sound's source. As the bat closes in on its *prey,* it increases its calling rate to a rapid-fire "feeding" buzz.

Using echolocation, this greater horseshoe bat trapped the moth with its wing and swept this bug meal into its mouth.

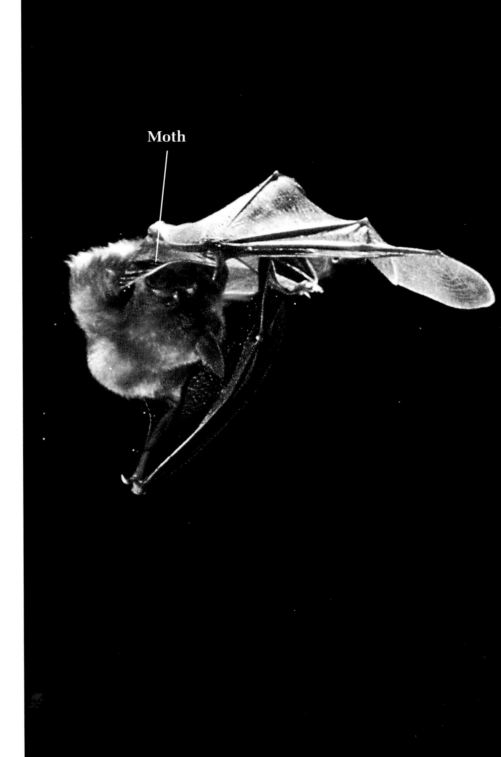

Moth

This greater bulldog bat's mouth is not open because it is fierce. It is calling as it flies low over the lake. It listens for echoes that let it detect ripples on the water—ripples made by a fish swimming near the surface. The bat swoops down, tracking the moving fish. Then, at just the right moment, the bat dips its big clawed feet into the water and snags the fish. The bat then quickly lifts the fish to its mouth. It may eat the fish in flight or carry it to a roost and dine while resting.

What big eyes the Peter's epauletted bat has! This bat used its eyes rather than its ears to find the fig it is eating. Then it sniffed to make sure the fig was ripe.

Some bats, like common vampire bats, have special smell sensors in the roof of their mouth to help them collect odors. You will remember that smell is also a way bats communicate, marking their roosts and mates with special scents.

Nectar-eating bats like this one often lack lower front teeth, making it easier for their long tongues to flick in and out.

Other bats, like certain long-nosed bats, depend on their sense of smell to find night-blooming flowers. These are usually stinky smells—the kind these bats love. Some *nectar*-feeding bats cling to the flowers to feed. Others, like the bat on page 3, hover, lapping up nectar with rapid-fire licks.

See the yellow dust on the bat's hair? This is *pollen,* the flower's male cells. If the bat then moves on to lick nectar from another flower of the same type of plant, the pollen is carried to the female part of this flower. When the male and female cells join, a seed is formed.

This common vampire bat is in mid-jump. Since this bat preys on animals much bigger than itself, it lands nearby and approaches with care. Vampire bats often hop around their prey before moving closer.

If its prey is hairy, the bat first shaves off the hair with its two razor-sharp front teeth.

The common vampire bat uses a combination of senses to find its animal prey, including echolocation, sight, and smell. It also has a special sensor on its nose that lets it detect warm animals by their body heat. Once the bat finds its prey, it does not kill and eat it. Instead, the bat bites and laps the animal's blood as it flows from a wound.

Most bats can fold their wings and use their thumbs, wrists, and feet to crawl or climb. Their hind legs, though, are long, thin, and weak—just right for helping control wing movements in flight. Vampire bats are unusual in having thicker, stronger hind legs. They can stand up on their hind legs and even jump to reach their prey.

Take a close look at the white-winged vampire bat dining on bird's blood. To start its meal, the bat bites and spits out the skin, making a shallow wound. Next, the bat laps to start the blood flowing. If you have ever had a cut or scrape, you have probably seen a scab form to stop the bleeding. The bat's spit has special chemicals that keep scabs from forming and the blood flowing. Grooves on the underside of the bat's tongue direct the blood into its mouth. To get enough to eat, the bat continues feeding for about eight minutes. Its full meal only amounts to about eight teaspoonfuls of blood, but that may equal 60 percent of the bat's body weight. To fly, the bat must somehow lighten its load.

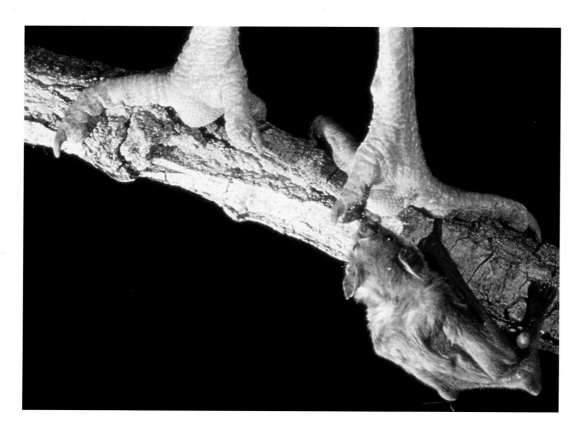

The feet don't belong to a giant bird; this white-winged vampire bat is very small.

As the blood fills the bat's *stomach,* the liquid part of the blood passes through the stomach lining and into the blood vessels. The two *kidneys,* special body parts that act as filters, quickly remove this excess liquid. Within two minutes of the time the vampire bat starts its blood meal, it begins to pass liquid waste. By the time it is ready to fly away, only *protein*-rich blood cells remain.

Female common vampire bats that roost together may line up to feed from the same wound. Back at the roost, if a hungry bat begs for food, a well-fed bat is likely to share by bringing up some of its blood meal.

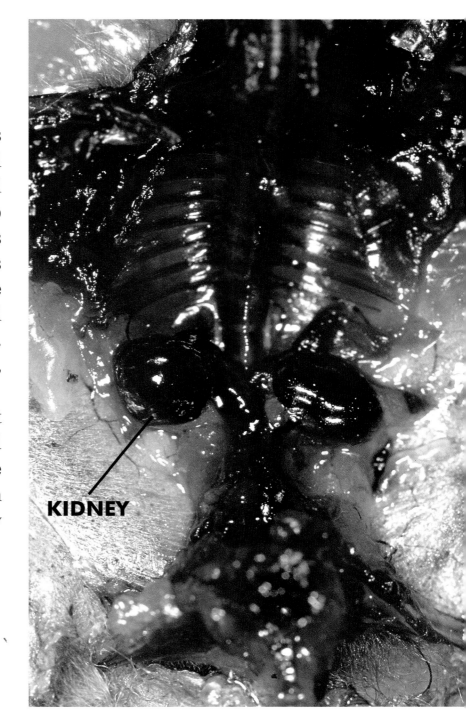

KIDNEY

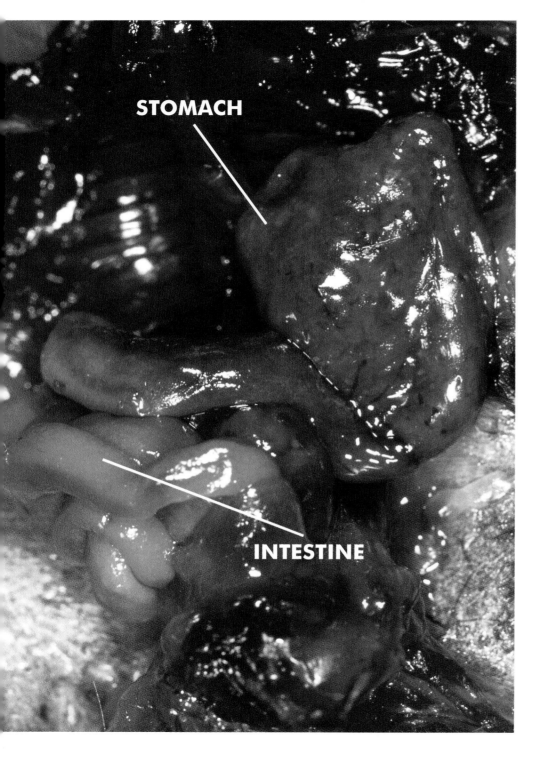

STOMACH

INTESTINE

Bats are likely to eat an amount of food equal to half their own body weight in a night. Some insect-eaters, like the big brown bat, may eat enough insects to equal their body weight. Imagine how much you would have to eat if you ate like a bat!

To stay light for flight, a bat chews food well before swallowing. Then it digests it quickly and promptly gets rid of solid wastes. It is not uncommon for a bat to digest its meal quickly and begin to pass both liquid and solid wastes within twenty minutes after eating. Most solid waste is passed within three or four hours after beginning to feed. After you eat, it takes your body from three to six hours to start using the food and more than a day to pass solid wastes.

Check out the W-shaped back teeth of this insect-eating <u>Nyctalus</u> bat. They're just right for crushing and slicing crunchy insects into a lumpy bug pudding.

Fruit-eaters, like the bat on page 18, suck while they chew, swallowing mostly easy-to-digest juice. Most fiber is spit out as a dry pellet. You can see what this is like by chewing a piece of celery until only the stringy fiber is left. Many fruit-eaters swallow small fruit whole—seeds and all.

Once the food is in the stomach, it is mixed with special juices that break down the food into its chemical building blocks called *nutrients.* In the *intestine,* the food nutrients pass into the bloodstream and are carried to all parts of the body.

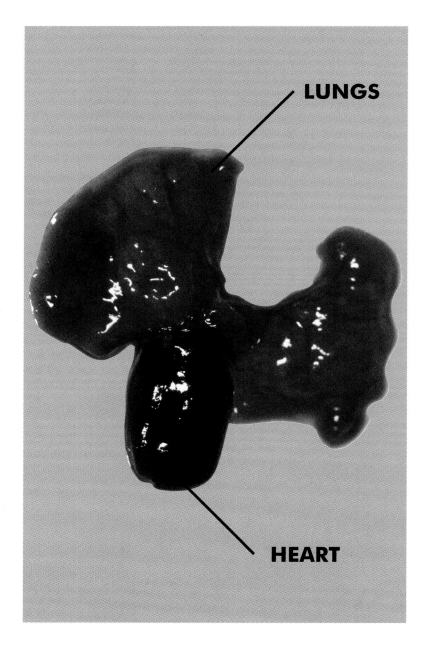

LUNGS

HEART

To make use of food nutrients, a bat needs a steady supply of *oxygen,* one of the gases in the air. Oxygen combines with the food nutrients to release the energy the bat needs to be active, stay warm, and grow. Like you, when a bat breathes in, air flows down the *windpipe* into the *lungs* where oxygen is exchanged for the waste gas *carbon dioxide.* Then the bat breathes out this waste gas.

The bat's blood carries oxygen and nutrients throughout its body. And the pump that pushes the blood is the *heart.* The heart is a muscle. But a bat does not control its heartbeat the way it does its wing flaps. The heart has a built-in pacemaker that keeps it beating. The brain controls how fast or slow the heart pumps—faster when it is active; slower when it is resting.

When bats are not flying they are resting to conserve energy. Do you wonder why bats rest hanging upside down? This makes it easy for the bat to take flight. It just lets go and flaps its wings.

Look at the Townsend's big-eared bat's knees. Bats are unique in having their legs rotated so the knees point backwards. This helps them steer in flight and makes it easier to hold their legs straight while resting. Usually, muscles must pull on bones to keep them straight, but when a bat hangs, its own weight and gravity do this job.

When most bats land, they flip in flight to grab hold upside down.

This greater horseshoe bat is not sleeping, it is hibernating. Bats that live where winters are too cold for their food to be available can only do two things: fly to warmer regions, like red bats and Mexican free-tailed bats do, or slow their energy use by hibernating. *Hibernation* is different than sleeping because the bat's body temperature drops to nearly that of the surrounding air—as low as just above freezing. Since producing body heat takes a lot of food energy, this lets the bat survive long periods without eating. Here you can see the greater horseshoe bat is wrapped in its wings, like snuggling in a blanket. Blood flow to the wings is also greatly reduced to prevent heat loss.

During hibernation, a bat's heart rate slows dramatically—for little brown bats, the rate drops from over a thousand beats per minute to as few as twenty-four beats per minute. The bat's breath rate slows so much that breaths may be separated by pauses lasting longer than a minute.

Water drops on the greater horseshoe bat's fur show that the air where this bat is hibernating is very humid. If the air was dry, the bat would lose needed water just by breathing. Then it would have to wake to drink.

Why do you think all these Eygptian fruit bats have crowded together?

Thousands of Mexican free-tailed bats roost together inside Bracken Cave in Texas. At dusk, they swarm out to search for dinner.

Did you guess the Egyptian fruit bats are sharing every inch of available roosting space inside the cave? Some kinds of bats prefer to rest alone in a tree or even under leaves. Others, like these Egyptian fruit bats, gather in caves or old mine tunnels to roost in large colonies. Sharing a shelter, though, does not make the bats any more of a group than people sharing an apartment building. Sometimes groups of females and groups of males will cluster separately. And sometimes, groups of females with babies gather in what are called nursery colonies. Baby bats are called pups.

Different kinds of bats mate during different times of the year. Those that live in tropical regions may mate and have babies more than once a year because there is plenty of food. Where winters get cold, some bats mate in late summer or fall, but the young do not begin to develop until spring. Whenever bats mate, a cell from the male, called a *sperm,* joins with the female's egg cell. Then the young, or *embryo,* develops inside the mother's body. As it grows, the embryo is attached inside its mother by a special cord through which it receives nutrients and oxygen. This is the way you developed too, but it took nine months before you were born. Most bat babies are born in fifty to one hundred days.

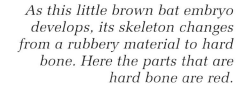

As this little brown bat embryo develops, its skeleton changes from a rubbery material to hard bone. Here the parts that are hard bone are red.

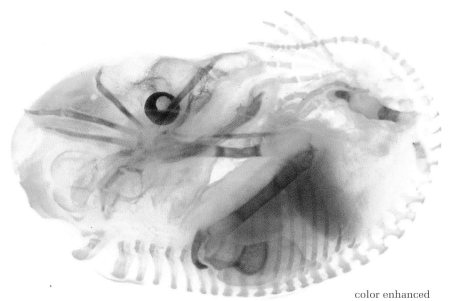

color enhanced

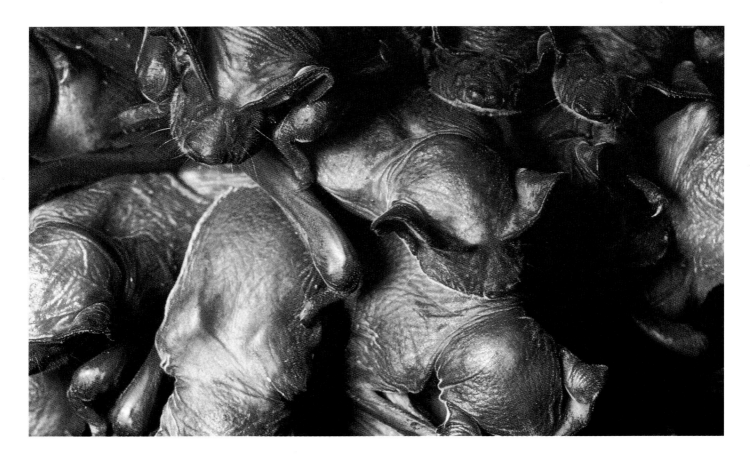

Some babies, like leaf-nosed bats, are born covered with hair and with their eyes open. Others, like these Mexican free-tailed bats, are born naked and have their eyes shut. The babies huddle together for warmth while waiting for their mothers to return from hunting. Like human mothers, bat mothers produce milk for their babies to suck from nipples.

Wonder how a mother bat finds her pup in this nursery? First the mother remembers the area in the cave where she left her baby. The mother gives a search call and listens. As she homes in on its answering peeps, the pup's odor lets her find her baby. Finding the right baby usually is not a problem even in the dark.

Even when it is not nursing, this young Egyptian fruit bat is warm and safe wrapped in its mother's wings. Mother bats and their babies are usually strongly bonded.

No one is sure how much mother bats train their young. But sac-winged bats have been seen following and mimicking how their mothers hunt and catch moths. Baby vampire bats have been seen feeding from a prey's wound opened by their mother.

Well fed and cared for, bat pups grow quickly. Just like you, young bats lose baby teeth and cut adult teeth. For bats, though, this happens when they are only about ten days old. Your adult teeth will not appear until you are at least six years old. By the time a bat baby is only four to six weeks old, it is ready to spread its wings and—with a little practice—fly and begin to feed on its own.

To prepare for its first flight, the youngster practices flapping its wings. If the bat is in a large shelter, like a cave, it next takes short flights within this safe space. Some mother bats, like <u>Nyctalus</u>, have been seen leading their babies on their first flight into the world. Other youngsters, like mouse-eared bats, are on their own from the start. Soon, though, all young bats are flying and hunting for themselves. Clearly, bats are special . . . from the inside out!

OPPOSITE PAGE: *This young Wahlberg's fruit bat is dining out with Mom in a fig tree.*

BUILD A BAT HOUSE

Some bats roost in boxes that people build especially for them. If you would like directions for building a bat house, write to Bat Conservation International and ask for a Bat House Builders Handbook (small fee required). The address is PO Box 162603, Austin, Texas 78716—or call 1-800-538-BATS.

This is a giant Indian flying fox.

LOOKING BACK

1. Look on page 5. How is the way the bluebird is landing different from the way a bat usually lands?

2. Check out the bat eating a fig on page 18. What is it using to hold on to the fig? Remember, its two front limbs support its wings.

3. What is the powdery stuff all over the faces of the bats on the title page? If you need a clue, read to find out what is on the face of the bat on page 19.

4. Look closely at the vampire bat's lower lip on page 21. How do you think its shape helps the bat lap up its blood meal?

5. How many bats can you count on page 29?

6. What is the flying fox on page 36 doing to make sure it will not fall out of the tree?

GLOSSARY/INDEX

BONES bōnz: The hard but lightweight parts that form the body's supporting frame. **9–11, 21, 27**

BRAIN brān: Body part that receives messages about what is happening inside and outside the body and that sends messages to put the body into action. **14, 26**

CARBON DIOXIDE kär´-bəndī-äk´-sīd: A gas that is given off naturally in body activities, carried to the lungs by the blood, and breathed out. **26**

CELLS selz: Tiny building blocks for all body parts. **14, 19, 31**

COLONY kol´-ə-nē: A group of bats sharing a shelter, such as a cave. **29–30**

ECHOLOCATION ek´-ō-lō-kā-shən: This is a method of navigating and finding food used by some bats. They produce blasts of high-pitched sound and then listen for the echoes that bounce off obstacles and other animals and back to them. **14–17, 21**

EMBRYO em´-brē-ō: Name given to the developing young. **31**

GLANDS glanz: Body parts that produce a particular substance for the bat's body. **8**

HEART härt: Body part that acts like a pump, constantly pushing blood throughout the bat's body. **26**

HIBERNATION hī´-bər-nā-shən: The inactive state which allows some kinds of bats to survive winters when their food supply is not available. During hibernation all body processes are greatly slowed. **28**

INTESTINE in-tes´-tin: The tube-shaped body part where food is mixed with special digestive juices to break it down into nutrients. The nutrients then pass through the walls into the bloodstream. **25**

KIDNEYS kid´-nēz: Body parts that remove wastes from blood. **23**

LIFT lift: An upward force that helps a bat fly. **12**

LUNG lung: Body part where oxygen and carbon dioxide are exchanged inside tiny, bubble-like air sacs. **26**

MEMBRANE mem´-brān: A thin tissue that serves as a covering or lining for a body organ or part. **6-8**

MUSCLES mə´-səls: Working in pairs, muscles move the bat's bones by pulling on them. **6, 10, 12, 15**

NECTAR nek´-tər: Sweet liquid produced in flowers to attract bats, insects, and birds. **19**

NOSE LEAVES noz lēvz: Elaborate facial parts that some bats have to help them direct pulses of sounds. The shape and arrangement of the nose leaves are different for different kinds of bats. **14**

NUTRIENTS nü´-trē-ənts: Chemical building blocks into which food is broken down for use by the bat's body. The five basic nutrients provided by foods are proteins, fats, carbohydrates, minerals, and vitamins. **25-26, 28**

OXYGEN äk´-si-jən: A gas in the air that is breathed into the lungs, carried by the blood to the cells, and combined with food nutrients to release energy. **26**

POLLEN päl´-ən: Produced by the male part of a flower, this contains the male cells or sperm. **19**

PREY prā: An animal or insect hunted by a bat. **20-21, 33**

PROTEIN prō´-tēn: Nutrient needed by animal bodies to build new cells and tissues. Because protein is not produced by animal bodies, it must be obtained from the food the animals eat. **23**

ROOST rōōst: A place where a bat anchors itself to rest. **8, 17-18, 23, 30**

SKELETON ske´-lə-tən: The framework of bones that supports the body and gives it its shape. **9-11**

SPERM spʉrm: The male reproductive cell. **31**

STOMACH stum´-ək: The stretchy body part able to store and break down food before it enters the intestine. **23, 25**

TONGUE tung: A movable muscle attached to the floor of the mouth. The bat uses its tongue to clean itself and carry food into the mouth. **14, 22**

WINDPIPE wind´-pīp: Tube that carries air from the nose and mouth to the lungs and back out again. **26**

WINGS wingz: Body part needed for flight. A bat's wings are made up of skin attached to the sides of its body and supported by the arms and fingers. Bats with long wingspans usually fly fast in open spaces; those with shorter wingspans are suited for making sharp turns and hovering in cluttered places. **5-7, 10, 12, 21, 26-27, 33-35**

ä as in c**a**rt	ā as in **a**pe	ə as in b**a**nan**a**	ē as in **e**ven	ī as in b**i**te
ō as in g**o**	ü as in r**u**le	ʉ as in f**u**r		

PHOTO CREDITS